BEN DRAWS TROUBLE

BY MATT DAVIES

A NEAL PORTER BOOK

ROARING BROOK PRESS

NEW YORK

For Lucy

A Neal Porter Book

Published by Roaring Brook Press

Roaring Brook Press is a division of Holtzbrinck Publishing Holdings Limited Partnership

175 Fifth Avenue, New York, New York 10010

The art for this book was created using pen and ink and watercolor on paper.

mackids.com

Library of Congress Cataloging-in-Publication Data

Davies, Matt (Matthew Keiland Parry), 1966–
  Ben draws trouble / Matt Davies. — First edition.
    pages cm
  "A Neal Porter Book."
  Summary: Ben loves to draw and does so in all of his classes, but his
drawings of people are so good he is afraid to let his classmates see
them, until the day he loses his notebook and his talent is revealed.
  ISBN 978-1-59643-795-1 (hardback)
[1. Drawing—Fiction. 2. Schools—Fiction. 3. Lost and found
possessions—Fiction. 4. Ability—Fiction.] I. Title.
  PZ7.D283825Bdr 2015
  [E]—dc23
                                2014009905

Roaring Brook Press books may be purchased for business or promotional use. For information
on bulk purchases please contact Macmillan Corporate and Premium Sales Department
at (800) 221-7945 x5442 or by email at specialmarkets@macmillan.com.

First edition 2015

Printed in China by Macmillan Production Asia Ltd., Kowloon Bay, Hong Kong (supplier code 10)

10 9 8 7 6 5 4 3 2 1

Ben Lukin loved
to draw in art class.

He loved to draw in writing class

and also in math class.

In fact, with a few pencil squiggles, he could make any classroom lesson . . .

just a teensy bit
more interesting.

But his teachers
didn't always agree.

Ben particularly enjoyed drawing bicycles,
motorcycles, boats, sharks, whales,
spaceships, dragons, monsters,
pizza, cars, guinea pigs,
dinosaurs, exotic reptiles,
crows, and . . .

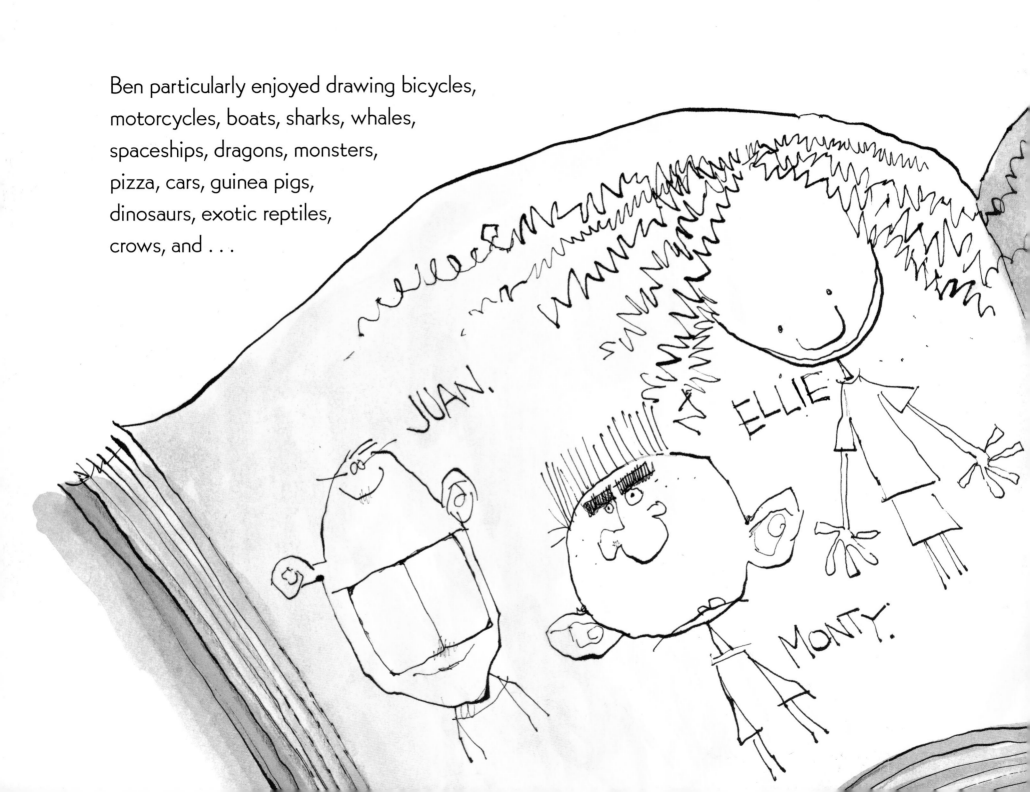

people.

Ben was very good
at drawing people . . .

maybe a little *too* good.

One day, while Ben was
riding home from school
(the long way, of course)
the unthinkable happened.

Upon arriving home,
Ben made himself a
nutritious snack.

Then, as always,
he reached for his sketchbook . . .

which appeared to
have been misplaced.

Meanwhile . . .

Ben looked everywhere,
until the sun stopped
cooperating and he went
home empty-handed.

The next morning, Ben raced to school—
the short way.

Perhaps he would find the sketchbook
left safely inside his desk.

As Ben
quietly tried
to slip away
he bumped
into his
teacher,
Mr. Upright,

who told him to find his seat.

Then something
(that had been thoughtfully
placed on his desk)
caught Mr. Upright's eye.

Mr. Upright looked inside,  lingered over a most interesting sketch of a tall man with a mustache,  and then noticed the cover.

After class, Mr. Upright led Ben toward the principal's office

and straight
past it.

Then Mr. Upright asked

if someone as talented as Ben
would be willing to help him.

Several months later, on opening night,
everyone at Watson Elementary agreed

that Ben's drawings
looked even better . . .

when they were twenty feet tall.